It's Good To Be Different

Story By N.J. Bernier   Pictures By J. Johnson

For my parents who urged me to read.

For my children who taught me, "It's good to be different".

On a gloomy winter day, Sigmund the duck was wandering and waddling around Brookside Farm. He looked confused. He looked sad. Sigmund was the only Indian Runner duck on the big farm. He looked lonely.

"Quack, quack," said Sigmund as he walked up to the sheep. They were Shetland Sheep from Scotland and they spoke with a lovely accent.
"Lilly?" quacked Sigmund.
"Yes," answered the ewe.
"Do I belong here?"

"Why, you're a duck, aren't ye laddie?"
"Yes."

"Well, there's a pond here in the pasture, so yes, you can stay here," she baa'd.
Sigmund thought about this for a moment. He didn't see any other ducks. He saw only sheep.

"Well," he thought to himself, "I must not belong here." He quietly thanked Lilly and waddled away. Once again, he looked sad.

This time, Sigmund came to the cows' field. He saw cows and calves eating hay. He saw a bull named Duke. Duke and the rest of the cows were Dexter cattle from Ireland. They also spoke with an accent.

He waddled up to Duke, who was a
nice dun colored cow with big horns.
"Excuse me, Duke?" quacked Sigmund.
"Yes, little duck, how may I help you?" bellowed the bull.
"I was wondering—do I belong here?"
Duke thought for a moment, then answered. "Yes, of course you
do! You can stay with us for as long as you like. There's a pond in the field
by the trees, plenty of food, and all the sunshine a duck could want."
"But," Sigmund started, "All you cows are so big. I'm so small. There is no
way I belong here." Before Duke could answer, Sigmund quickly waddled
away.

He felt even more alone than ever before. How could he possibly belong with the cows or the sheep? They were so different. He was small, he had brown and white feathers, and he had webbed feet. They all had brown, black, and white fur. They had hooves and were so much bigger. He couldn't possibly belong here.

As he was walking along, he came across a gaggle of geese. These were Pilgrim geese that are on the endangered species list. They are extremely rare and extremely loud!

"Honk," yelled one of the ganders. "Watch out duck! We have cracked corn to eat."
"Oh sorry," quacked Sigmund.
"You can eat some of the corn too," said one of the blue-gray females. Her name was Sassy.
"I can? Do I belong here?" asked Sigmund.
"Sure, you can stay with us little duck. We have plenty of corn, a nice little pond to swim in, and a good spot for shelter when it gets too cold.

"But you all are so much bigger. You're from Iowa and I am from Malaysia, so I must not belong here either," Sigmund quickly waddled away before Sassy could answer.

He went by the chicken coop and he was going to ask if he belonged there. He saw Speckled Sussex, Rhode Island Reds, Buff Orpingtons, Dominiques, and Barred Rocks. They were all different colors, sizes and spoke with different accents. There was even a Catalana rooster from the Mediterranean with brightly colored plumage.
"Well, I can't possibly belong here," said Sigmund.

He decided there was nothing left to do but leave Brookside Farm. He had no belongings and no pockets anyway, so he started to waddle down the driveway. He looked back one last time and started to cry. He was going to miss all the other animals (even the cats who always kept their eye on him). He was going to miss the human food bringers, because they were always nice, too. So, he turned and headed down the drive way.

"Hey kid! Where are you headed off to?" asked a familiar voice.
"Hi Marley," said Sigmund to the dog. Sigmund had forgotten to ask the dogs! They were so smart and always knew what to do. They were always helping the sheep or cows get into their pens or into different fields.
"Where are you going?" asked Marley.
"I'm leaving the farm. I don't belong here," said Sigmund moping.

"What do you mean you don't belong?"

"No one is like me. I am completely different than all the other animals, even though they said I could stay with them," he cried.

"But that's what makes you so wonderful, Sigmund. And that is what is so great about Brookside Farm. You being different from the rest of us is what makes you so special."

"It is?" asked Sigmund, his tears gone.

"Yes. That is what makes the whole world so special. There are three Australian shepherds and one Labrador retriever here on the farm. Talk about diversity! Our black Labrador is from Canada, we Aussies come from the American west and our breeds are all kinds of colors. I'm a red tri, we have a black tri and a blue merle here at Brookside and there are even red merles on other farms. But we are one pack and we help the animals together."

"Without diversity, it would be a boring place. Not just us animals, but among humans too. Did you know that humans come in different colors?"

"They do?" asked Sigmund.

"Of course, little duck. No one person or animal looks the same. That's why this world is so amazing."

"Wow," he said, amazed.

"So you see Sigmund, you do belong here. Brookside Farm is your world and your difference from others is not so different after all. Do you understand?"

"I think so, Marley. No matter what any animal or human looks like, they all belong together, they can all coexist, and they can all live together in harmony. So it's good to be different.

"That's right kid," said Marley, smiling.

"It's good to be different," shouted Sigmund.

"It's good to be different," barked Marley.

Off in the distance, Sigmund heard all the other animals shouting his phrase, "it's good to be different". It came from the sheep pasture, then it came from the cow fields then the geese honked out their repetition of the phrase. Then the chickens did so and the cats could also be heard. The dogs howled the phrase. Sigmund smiled as he walked back towards home, where his friends were welcoming him.
"It's good to be different", they all said together.

The End